Miss Opal's Auction

SUSAN VIZURRAGA

illustrated by MARK GRAHAM

HENRY HOLT AND COMPANY — NEW YORK

Henry Holt and Company, LLC, *Publishers since 1866*
115 West 18th Street, New York, New York 10011

Henry Holt is a registered
trademark of Henry Holt and Company, LLC

Text copyright © 2000 by Susan Vizurraga
Illustrations copyright © 2000 by Mark Graham
All rights reserved.
Published in Canada by Fitzhenry & Whiteside Ltd.,
195 Allstate Parkway, Markham, Ontario L3R 4T8.

Library of Congress Cataloging-in-Publication Data
Vizurraga, Susan.
Miss Opal's auction / by Susan Vizurraga; illustrated by Mark Graham.
Summary: As the contents of Miss Opal's house are auctioned off before she moves to
a retirement home, Annie recalls all the things they did together, from baking cookies and
making ice cream to listening to ball games on the radio.
[1. Old age—Fiction.   2. Auctions—Fiction.   3. Afro-Americans—Fiction.]
I. Graham, Mark, ill.   II. Title.
PZ7.V85Mi   2000   [E]—dc21   99-33610

ISBN 0-8050-5891-5 / First Edition—2000
Printed in the United States of America on acid-free paper. ∞
The artist used oil on canvas to create the illustrations for this book.
1   3   5   7   9   10   8   6   4   2

For my children
and in memory of my grandmothers,
Verona Rogler Pluckhan and Marguerite Aubrey Dean
—S. V.

To Marie
—M. G.

"*Going once . . .*
going twice . . .
SOLD!
To number seventeen!"
the auctioneer shouted.

A woman in a polka-dot dress
waved a paper plate in the air.
The ladies sitting on Miss Opal's front porch
rocked back in their chairs
and smiled behind their fans.
I could tell they thought
the woman had paid too much
for that rusty blue scooter.
Even I knew that it always pulled to the right,
no matter which foot you put on it.
But that woman wasn't paying any mind to them.
She was looking in her checkbook
to see if she could buy some more
of Miss Opal's nice old things.

Next the auctioneer picked up
the big radio with the wooden case
that Miss Opal listened to
for gospel music and the morning farm report.
On Saturdays she'd let me
tune in the baseball game,
while she baked pies
and I shooed the flies away.
The radio buzzed and crackled
and gave everything a fuzzy sound.
It seemed like all she had was from long ago—
and Miss Opal was, too.
She had been old,
real old, for as long as I could remember.

She used to go out more,
bringing pound cakes and tomatoes
to the neighbors who could use them.
But lately Miss Opal had been staying
around her white clapboard house,
and I was there to help her.
"Just a few minutes is all you need to stay,"
my mama would say.
But on the days we were gardening or cooking
and Miss Opal got to talking,
I could listen the whole afternoon.

The auctioneer was holding up
Miss Opal's ice-cream churn.

"It's an old one, but it works, folks.
Do I hear ten?
Ten dollars, ten dollars.
I've got ten dollars.
Do I hear twelve? . . ."

It was just last summer
when I brought Miss Opal
a bucket of blackberries
I'd picked from along her fence.
"These berries are begging for ice cream," she said,
and she got out her recipe book and mixed some up,
and I used the hammer to crack the ice.
We took turns cranking that old churn
and ate blackberries and ice cream
while it was still soft and mushy.

"SOLD!
For fifteen dollars!"
the auctioneer shouted,
and then the ice-cream churn was gone.
As the auctioneer's voice ran on,
I kept my eye on Miss Opal.
She sat in a straight-backed kitchen chair,
fanning herself and half listening
to the other ladies gossiping on her porch.
But all the time Miss Opal watched
as her old things were sold.

I bet it was sad
for Miss Opal to see her belongings
leaving in the hands of neighbors and strangers,
but I knew the auction
was her own idea.

Miss Opal had found a new home,
an apartment in a big building
where a lot of older people live.
"I'm choosing a place now," she said,
"while I've still got sense enough to choose it myself.
Besides, I won't have room for all these things there."
Miss Opal winked at me and smiled.
"And where I'm going after that,
Lord knows I can't take them with me."

I stood at the edge of the porch
and watched all the people
scattered around the folding chairs
on Miss Opal's front lawn,
and I looked at the stacks
of Miss Opal's old things.

The woman in the polka-dot dress
was studying Miss Opal's rickety kitchen cabinet,
checking the latches
and pulling out the drawers.
In one, there was a yellowed seed catalogue
that Miss Opal and I looked at in January
when we planned her spring vegetable garden.
I filled in the tiny lines on the order form,
and she sent me out to her mailbox every day
to see if the seeds had come.
Corn and tomatoes,
okra, onions, peppers, summer squash—
Miss Opal had recipes to make them all taste good.

An antiques dealer
(that's what I heard the old ladies call him)
poked around the boxes and furniture
lined up in the grass.
There were boxes full of old Mason jars
from when Miss Opal put up
her peaches and tomatoes and strawberry jam.
Jars of preserves
used to line the shelves of her pantry.
But now I filled the empty jars with flowers
from the corners of her yard
where Miss Opal doesn't walk anymore.

Crash!
What sounded like a cymbal
was the top from an old cookie tin
that the antiques dealer had picked up to inspect.
There was a whole box full of the tins
that Miss Opal and I filled
with the cookies we baked at Christmas—
sugar cookies with colored frosting,
thumbprint cookies filled with jam,
and gingerbread people
with raisin eyes and licorice string ties.

In her cookbook Miss Opal wrote notes
next to my favorite recipes:
"Annie likes this one"
or "extra frosting for Annie H."
And when I looked through that cookbook
I read more notes scratched in the margins—
"less sugar next time,"
"Henry loves this one,"
"Mother's favorite casserole," and
"good for church supper."
I wondered if that recipe book
was in one of those boxes
stacked on Miss Opal's front lawn.

I heard everyone talking and laughing,
the old ladies telling stories on Miss Opal's porch,
and the auctioneer's patter in the background.
"SOLD for fifty dollars,"
the auctioneer bellowed,
and I saw the antiques dealer
step forward to claim the box he'd bought.
He ran his hand across the top layer of books
and lifted one out.
It was Miss Opal's recipe book.

Suddenly my stomach felt like a knot,
and I needed a place to hide.
I ducked under the drooping branches
of Miss Opal's magnolia tree
and stood inside the tent the tree made for me.
Her recipes were gone,
and soon she would be, too.

Miss Opal was really leaving,
going off to her retirement home,
and we wouldn't be baking or gardening
or just talking anymore.
I didn't even know
if I'd ever see her again.

I blinked hard
and looked out between the magnolia leaves.
Miss Opal was talking to the antiques dealer
and taking some money from her pocket.
The man counted the dollar bills
as Miss Opal walked toward me,
holding the old cookbook against her chest.
She stepped carefully between the folding chairs
and stood outside the magnolia tent.
"I think you're the one who should have this,"
she said as she held out the book.

Miss Opal and I sat
in the last row of folding chairs
and watched the people milling about on her lawn.
We watched all her things loaded into cars
and pickup trucks.
When the auctioneer and his wife
started folding up the chairs,
it was time for me to say good-bye.
Miss Opal took my hand and patted it,
and I walked away with her cookbook
held tight against my chest.

Sometimes I think about that day
at Miss Opal's auction.
But mostly I think about the times
we spent together talking and gardening
and cooking in her kitchen.
And sometimes I get out
Miss Opal's cookbook and Mama and I
work on one of her recipes.
We follow her directions,
and I remember Miss Opal
when I smell those cookies baking.
And just as they did
when Miss Opal was here,
those cookies sure taste good.